For Bertie

First American edition, 1989.
Text and illustrations copyright © 1989 by Deborah van der Beek.
All rights reserved. Published simultaneously in Canada.
Originated and published in Great Britain by Piccadilly Press, 1989.
Printed in Belgium by Proost International Book Production
Library of Congress Cataloging-in-Publication Data
van der Beek, Deborah. Superbabe at the park.
Summary: Superbabe's visit to the park playground leaves everyone exhausted.
[1. Babies – Fiction.   2. Stories in rhyme]
I.   Title PZ8.3.V33Sug 1989 [E] 88-32331
ISBN 0-399-21750-9
G.P. Putnam's Sons, 200 Madison Avenue, NYC 10016
First impression

SUPERBABE
at the Park

by Deborah van der Beek

G. P. Putnam's Sons
New York

See his fingers,
See his thumbs,
See my brother,
Here he comes!

Yes, here he is.
It's Superbabe!
The fastest thing on knees.

Bootees, mittens,
Scarf and hat,
Must you wear all these . . .

. . . for a trip to the park on such a warm day?

Can I have an ice cream?

Can we feed the ducks, Mom?

But Superbabe has to have it his way.

Can I have a drink?

Tell me what you think.

Once in the park,
He looks all around,
This way and that.
And heads for . . .

. . . the playground.

We put him on the swing,

He laughs and laughs until we stop,

We put him in the sandbox; he makes a sandy pie.

And swing him really high.

And then he starts to cry.

First he eats the sand up, then gets it in his eye.

Up the slide we climb.
And down again we go.
Whizzing, zizzing, faster, faster.
We don't like it slow!

Come on! Come on!
He's off again,
What does he want to see?

I know! I know!
The thing with holes,
Is where he wants to be!

The thing with holes?

It's a horse.   It's a house.

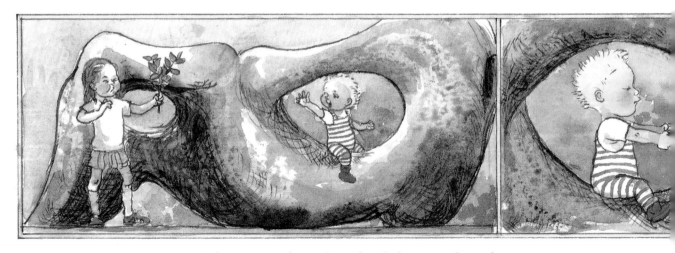

It's a train that's his and mine.

Ah, the Thing with Holes!

I'm a cat.   He's a mouse.

(Even though the sign below says "Figure in Recline.")

Look at the ducks Mom,
Up there in the sky!
Let's go and feed them.
Their pond must be nearby.

No, Superbabe! Superbabe!
That's not what you do.
The bread is for ducks.
It isn't for you!

Hey, if you wriggle like that,
You'll lose your hat!
(But he isn't wearing his hat . . .)

Superbabe!
Where are all your clothes?
Your mittens,
Your scarf,
Your bootees,
Your hat?
"Oh no," groaned my Mom,
"He's even lost that."

And then Mom says wearily,
Before he's all undressed,
Let's all go to the coffee shop,
I think I need a rest.

Can we have an ice cream?
The kind with chocolate crunch?
*I'm sorry, dear – and Superbabe.
You won't want any lunch.*

Ba-Ba-Ba!   Mmm?

Ooh!   Gggh!   Bzzzz!

But what is this? Did he say "hat"?

Baa?   Bzz.   Bll?   Gah!

Grrr.   *Superbabe!*   *Maria!*   Eee?

It's a word! It's a word!   It's his very first word!

Mom, look at that
It's Superbabe's hat!

Clever Maria saw them fall,
She didn't miss a thing at all:
Mittens, bootees, scarf, and hat,
See if you can find all that.

One by one, he dropped his clothes,
From the top of his head, to the tip of his toes.
Look back and see if you can find,
Just where he left his things behind . . .

Mom, can we have an ice cream?
The kind with chocolate crunch?
*Well, I think we need to celebrate,
So shall we stay for lunch?*

PRINTED IN BELGIUM BY

proost

INTERNATIONAL BOOK PRODUCTION